The cat with two homes

A first book of opposites

Written by Tim Healey
Illustrated by Jo Burroughes

PUBLISHED BY THE READER'S DIGEST ASSOCIATION LIMITED

Olly was a stray cat – and a very ordinary cat at that. His coat was no particular colour: a sort of greyish, brownish, stripy tabby. He was not especially thin or fat or especially big or small. Olly was, well, ordinary.

But Olly the Ordinary Cat had
seen enough of the world to know
that it can be an extraordinary
place. For example, at some
times of year the weather is hot . . .

. . . and at other times it is cold.

Some places for snoozing are
rather soft . . .

. . . and others are hard.

Some dogs run very fast . . .

. . . and others are very slow.

Some places are noisy . . .

. . . and others are quiet.

Often, as he prowled around the
streets and gardens of his town,

Olly would find windows shut . . .

But sometimes he would find a
window open.

And sometimes he would sneak
inside to look about.

One day, Olly slipped into the home of the Tubbs family. It was very untidy in there.

"Eek!" squealed Mrs Tubbs.

"There's a cat in the living room.
Look, everyone, look!"
"Don't frighten the poor thing,"
said Mr Tubbs. "He looks
hungry. Here, puss, puss . . ."
"I wasn't trying to frighten him,
dear," said Mrs Tubbs. "I
merely said, 'Eek'. But you're
right. That cat has not been
properly fed." And she went off
to the kitchen to see what food
she could find.

The Tubbs were short and chubby.

They were a kind family, too,
and from that day onward they
allowed Olly to make their house
his home.

Every morning, Olly dropped in
and was given an enormous
breakfast. The Tubbs thought of
Olly as a rather skinny cat and
they laid out huge amounts of food.

There was much more than Olly could eat, and he was always so full up that he left some of it.

The Tubbs did not know Olly's real name so they decided to call him "Slim". They even bought a feeding dish and wrote the name upon it.

Olly the Ordinary Cat did not spend the whole day hanging around the Tubbs' house. He liked to roam, and around midday he would often find himself near the home of the Pyke family who lived in the same street, but on the opposite side of the road.

One day, Olly had a fight with a neighbour's cat and hid in the Pykes' garden to lick his wounds.

Mrs Pyke found him there and
brought him into the house.

"Look at this poor stray," Mrs Pyke said to her husband. "See, he's been in a fight and he needs someone to look after him." "Hrumph," said Mr Pyke. "He looks well enough looked after to me. Just see what a plump fellow he is. A real old roly-poly."

The Pykes' house was quite unlike the Tubbs' home. It was very tidy.

And the Pykes themselves were
both rather tall and thin.

They were a kindly family, and they did not like to think of Olly having no home to go to. From that day onward they gave Olly the freedom of their house.

Every lunchtime, Olly would drop in and was given a midday meal. The Pykes thought of Olly as rather a plump cat, and only laid out tiny quantities of food.

"That cat," said Mrs Pyke, "is much too fat – but we can't give him nothing at all."

And because the Pykes did not know Olly's real name, they called him "Podge". They even bought him a feeding dish and wrote the name upon it.

So it was that Olly became a Cat with Two Homes. For many years he lived in or about the same neighbourhood without anyone suspecting his secret. Until, one afternoon – one very ordinary afternoon – Mr and Mrs Tubbs met Mr and Mrs Pyke in the street. Olly happened to be snoozing on a wall nearby.

"Look at the lazy creature," said Mrs Tubbs fondly. "He's our cat, you know – always comes by for breakfast. We call him 'Slim'!"

"But he's *our* cat," said the
astonished Mrs Pyke. "He has
his lunch with us. We call him
'Podge'!"

"A cat with two homes!"
chuckled Mr Tubbs.

"A cat with two names!"
laughed Mr Pyke.

And their laughter wakened Olly
from his sleep. He licked his lips
and yawned. Then he stretched
himself, so that he looked very
long and thin . . .

. . . then he puffed out his fur so that he looked rather short and fat.

And then he darted off. He
jumped over one garden gate . . .

. . . he sneaked under another.

He climbed up onto a roof . . .

. . . and down the other side.

He dashed into a big drainpipe . . .

. . . and came out of the other end.

Where was he going? Well, because it was late afternoon and would soon be time for his evening meal, Olly was going off to eat at his third home.
Third home?

Oh yes, didn't I tell you? Olly has a third home – and it's the one he likes best of all. It must be a really snug home, too, for he goes there every night.

But where is that home?
It's a secret known only to Olly.

... it's a bit of a mystery to me.

MY WONDERFUL WORDBOX

First Edition Copyright © 1989
The Reader's Digest Association Limited,
Berkeley Square House, Berkeley Square,
London W1X 6AB
Reprinted 1990

® READER'S DIGEST, THE DIGEST and
the Pegasus logo are registered trademarks of
The Reader's Digest Association, Inc.
of Pleasantville, New York, U.S.A.

Printed in Hong Kong